S0-ALG-067

THE EXTRAORDINARY FILES

Sleepwalker

Paul Blum

HAMERAY
PUBLISHING GROUP

"The truth is inside us.
It is the only place where it can hide."

Published in the United States of America
by the Hameray Publishing Group, Inc.

Text © Rising Stars UK Ltd.
Published 2008
Author: Paul Blum
Editorial Consultants: Adria Klein, Lorraine Petersen

Cover design: Button plc
Illustrator: Aleksandar Sotiroski
Text design and typesetting: pentacorbig
Publisher: Gill Budgell
Project management and editorial: Lesley Densham
Editor: Maoliosa Kelly

All rights reserved. No part of this publication may be reproduced or
transmitted in any form or by any means without permission in writing from
the publisher. Reproduction of any part of this book, through photocopy,
recording, or any electronic or mechanical or retrieval system without the
written permission of the publisher, is an infringement of the copyright law.

ISBN 978-1-60559-021-9

Printed in Singapore.

1 2 3 4 5 PP 12 11 10 09 08

CHAPTER ONE

It was the middle of the night in Baltimore, Maryland. All the houses on Ronald Terrace were quiet, except for number four. There was shouting and screaming coming from one of the upstairs bedrooms.

An eighteen-year-old girl was holding a knife over the bed of her sleeping mother. Two men were pulling her back. One was her father, Mr. Warner. The other was a policeman.

"This is the work of the devil," said Mr. Warner.

The policeman put handcuffs on the girl.

"Look at her eyes. She's fast asleep," he said.

"Don't be fooled. The devil has many tricks," replied Warner.

FBI Headquarters, Washington, D.C.

Agent Laura Turnbull went into
Agent Robert Parker's office at
FBI headquarters.

"What a mess! How can you work
like this?" she asked.

"I know where everything is," replied
Agent Parker.

"And it stinks!" Turnbull pushed some
trash off a chair.

Parker's face went red.

"Do you want to hear what I've got
on this new Warner case?" he asked.

"Get up, please," she said.

"Pardon?"

"I want your seat."

"Do you want to see the computer?"
Parker asked.

"No, I don't want to get my new suit
dirty on this chair."

Parker looked through his papers and then said, "Warner is a preacher."

"Go on."

"He is a prime time TV preacher. His ratings are sky high. Millions of people think he is wonderful."

"So what is his attraction?"

"He can predict the future and talk to the dead."

"Is he a fake?" asked Turnbull.

Robert Parker drank his coffee. "Yes, probably. The government loves him. As so many millions watch him, it's like a free advertisement for the government."

"So what's the problem then?"

Parker clicked a button on the computer. It showed a picture of a young woman. "She is. This is his daughter, Amanda Warner."

"Pretty girl," Turnbull said.

"She keeps trying to kill her mother. Mr. Warner is blaming the devil," said Parker.

"I don't see what any of this has got to do with us," said Turnbull sharply.

"Orders from high up. Warner is sounding crazier and crazier by the minute."

"So what?"

"Some people in high places don't like that. Warner is always saying the government is wonderful but who wants the support of a madman?
The government wants him stopped."

"So our job is . . ." Turnbull said.

"To go and see Warner and his daughter. Find out what is going on and put a stop to it as quickly as possible."

CHAPTER TWO

The agents arrived at the big house belonging
to the Warners.

The rooms were full of strange objects.
There was a big fish tank in the living room.
Mr. Warner came into the room.

"Agents Turnbull and Parker, I have been
expecting you," he said.

Parker smiled and shook his hand. He started
off with a bit of flattery. "It's our pleasure. I've
seen you on television. I hardly ever miss a
show."

"I am glad you have listened to my message,"
said Warner.

Parker looked around the room. He patted his
little notebook. "I need to talk to your daughter
Amanda alone. Agent Turnbull will want to ask
you some questions."

Warner laughed. He had a very loud laugh.
The agents stood back a bit. The laugh was
strange and frightening.

"Yes, of course, detectives," he said. "We have
nothing to hide. Let me get Amanda."

Parker was surprised when he saw Amanda. She was beautiful but her eyes looked restless and wild.

Parker and Amanda went out into the garden.

"Your father says you can hear voices," Parker said.

"Yes, I can. In my head," replied Amanda.

"Did you hear the voices before you attacked your mother?" asked Parker.

"I can't remember anything. All I remember is waking up in my bed," said Amanda.

"Do you sleepwalk?"

"Yes. Since I was a child."

"Sleepwalkers are often worried about something in their lives. Are you?"

Amanda pushed back her lovely long hair. She gave him a very long stare.

"Right now I am only worried about one thing," she said.

"And what's that?"

"About wanting to kiss you," she said.

Parker was surprised. He dropped his notebook into a flower bed, then took a step back.

"You hardly know me, Amanda," he said.

"I knew you as soon as I saw you, Agent Parker," said Amanda.

"But we have only been talking for ten minutes."

"Agent Parker, do you like me?"

"What kind of question is that? I am a detective. You are supposed to be answering *my* questions."

"Well, do you? Be honest with me, Agent Parker."

Miss Warner moved towards him and he ran back into the house.

The investigation had hit a problem.

CHAPTER THREE

Later that day, Parker and Turnbull drove to a hospital.
They were going to meet Dr. Smith, a world expert on
sleeping problems.

There were electric fences all around the hospital.

"High security," said Parker.

"They are not the only ones who need it, Parker."

"What do you mean?"

"Perhaps we should lock you up here so you can be safe from Amanda."

"Agent Turnbull that's not funny!"

"Agent Parker, you are right. It isn't funny. But we have learned one useful thing."

"What?"

"Amanda Warner is definitely crazy if she likes you," laughed Turnbull.

Agent Parker looked upset
but he tried to smile.

They went in through the gate
of the hospital. Doctor Smith
met them and took them on a
tour of the hospital.

"Are the people here prisoners
or patients?" asked Turnbull.

"Some of them are here for
a very long time. With first
degree murder you stay here
at a judge's pleasure," said
Doctor Smith.

"We could keep Agent Parker
here for Amanda's pleasure,"
laughed Turnbull.

Parker gave her a hurt look.

They looked through the peephole of one cell. They saw a young girl crying. She was rocking from side to side on her bed.

"This is Tracy. She is in a terrible state," said the doctor.

Turnbull looked upset. "What's wrong with her?"

"She hears voices in her head."

"What do they tell her?" asked Turnbull.

"To kill herself. A punishment for what she did."

"What did she do?"

The doctor whispered, "She attacked her mother's boyfriend. Killed him. Tied him up in a sack. She was only fourteen at the time but she remembers nothing," continued Doctor Smith.

Turnbull was surprised. "Nothing?" she asked.

"She was sleepwalking at the time."

"Sleepwalking?"

Turnbull was deep in thought before she said, "I think we have a similar case."

"Then be careful. Sleepwalkers have no control over what they are doing. Drugs can calm them down but the wrong drugs can make them even more violent."

Doctor Smith took the agents into his office. It was full of television screens with videos. From the office he could watch every patient in the hospital, twenty-four hours a day.

"We get early warning from these pictures. We look for sudden changes in behavior. It keeps my staff as safe as they can be," he said.

"They are very deadly men and women," said Turnbull.

"Deadly!" said the doctor.

CHAPTER FOUR

Agent Turnbull went back to number four Ronald Terrace.

She went up to Mrs. Warner's bedroom. Mrs. Warner looked pale and ill. Turnbull knew that the questions she had to ask would only make her feel worse.

"Thanks for seeing me, Mrs. Warner. Sorry to disturb you like this."

Agent Turnbull took a letter out of her bag.
She handed it to Mrs. Warner. "Have you seen this
before?" she asked.

Mrs. Warner read it slowly. "It's a bill for $20,000.
Where did you get it?" she asked the agent.

"I found it in your trash can."

"Well, I've already paid it," Mrs. Warner said.

"But it's a bill for a gambling debt, Mrs. Warner.
Do you gamble?"

"No, of course I don't."

"So who does? Is it your husband?"

"My husband is a good man. He would never do a
thing like that."

Turnbull saw the tears in Mrs. Warner's eyes. She
thanked Mrs. Warner for her help and left the house.

Mr. Warner shut the door behind Turnbull. After she had gone, he went into his study. He took out of his desk some glass tubes full of chemicals. The phone rang.

"Look, leave me alone. You will get your money!" he shouted.

He slammed down the phone and then picked it up again.

"Amanda darling, come and see your daddy now."

Amanda came down from her bedroom.

"Amanda, sit down here. I've got some bad news for you," said Warner.

"Daddy, what are you talking about?"

"You know Agent Parker," he said.

"Agent Parker. You mean Robert?"

"I have heard something about him, my dear."

"What sort of thing?" she asked, in a worried voice.

"That he's in love with Agent Turnbull."

"Don't be so silly. It must be a lie," Amanda cried. "You are always trying to hurt me. Just leave me alone."

Amanda ran out of the room, crying.

Back at Parker's office, the two agents had been looking into the Warner's money. Turnbull did a little math in her notebook.

"He owes almost four million dollars," she said.

Parker looked surprised. "But he earns a fortune!"

Turnbull went on talking.

"His television company belongs to Mrs. Warner. She is the one with the money. And she is the one with the big life insurance policy. If she dies, he gets loads of money. Even better if his daughter gets a life sentence for her murder. That gets everybody out of the way. Very clever!"

Mr. Warner: owes $4,000,000

Mrs. Warner: owns TV company

has life insurance policy

Amanda: murder; life sentence

Parker was shocked. He looked at his computer screen. "It's too clever. We don't have any proof. Why shouldn't we believe that Amanda is evil? Maybe she really is a girl with murder on her mind."

The phone rang. It was Warner.

"Come quickly, Agent Parker. The full moon is high and the devil is nigh!"

"I beg your pardon, sir," said Parker.

"Amanda is sleepwalking. She has a knife."

"We are on our way!" shouted Parker.

Parker and Turnbull jumped into the car.

Turnbull was not happy. "I am getting too old for this kind of thing," she said.

"Nonsense, Turnbull, you are as fit as a fiddle."

"Is that a compliment, Parker?"

"Yes."

"Or are you just hoping I will look after you if there is any rough stuff?"

"You know me. I hate fighting," he said.

"You are such a wimp, Parker."

"Not like you, Turnbull."

"Just as well, isn't it? Somebody's got to wear the pants around here. Now drive as fast as you can. It's an emergency and we are secret agents!"

CHAPTER FIVE

They got out of the car and tiptoed to the Warner's house.

Everything was dark and quiet. There was a feeling of danger in the air. The front door was open. Turnbull tried the light.

"The power is off," she said.

"Oh no. I think we should go," said Parker.

"Get a grip, Parker. This is important. Somebody's life may be in danger."

"Yeah, mine."

"Ssssh," she hissed.

They heard footsteps upstairs. Turnbull pulled a flashlight out of her bag. They went up the steps.

Warner was standing outside his daughter's bedroom. He was holding a small glass of water. Turnbull shined the flashlight in his face.

"What do you think you are doing?" she shouted.

"Agent Turnbull, I can feel the devil."

"What is in that glass?" she asked.

"Holy water."

33

"Where is your wife?" Parker demanded.

"I have locked her in the bedroom. She's safe."

"I will fix the lights," Parker said. "Where is your fuse box?"

"In the cellar."

Parker went downstairs, leaving Turnbull and Warner alone.

Suddenly they heard a voice on the other side of the door.

"It's Amanda. She is banging her head against the wall! We have to break the door down before she hurts herself," Turnbull shouted.

Warner gave Turnbull a strange look and shouted to Amanda through the door.

"Amanda, Agent Turnbull is here. Will you open the
door? Amanda, Amanda, can you hear us?"

The door opened. Turnbull shined the flashlight into the room. She saw Amanda standing there. Suddenly Amanda screamed. Something hit Turnbull over the head and she passed out.

Down in the cellar, Parker had found the fuse box.
As he fixed the lights, the door slammed shut.
He was trapped!

CHAPTER SIX

Mr. Warner took his daughter by the arm and led her towards Agent Turnbull.

"She must die. She took Agent Parker away from you."

Warner put a knife into the sleeping girl's hand and held it over Turnbull's body.

"After her, Amanda, there is much work for you to do," he whispered in her ear.

Just then, Parker burst into the room. He pushed Amanda to the floor. Warner ran away.

Parker shook Turnbull who was beginning to move.

"How are you feeling?" he said.

"Like I just got hit over the head with a hammer."

"And you did."

"Why are you standing over me like that?" she asked.

"I just saved your life."

"You're joking."

"Amanda was about to kill you with a knife."

39

They ran down the hallway.

When they got to Mrs. Warner's bedroom Turnbull kicked in the door. Warner was there. He had a big needle on a tray.

"I was expecting you two," he said.

"You were?" said Parker.

Warner laughed loudly. "I have something special for both of you."

He grabbed the needle and ran towards them. Parker dived behind the chair and Turnbull managed to kick the needle out of Warner's hand. Then she got him in an armlock and swung him around.

"And I have something special for you too," she said.

Parker crawled from behind his chair and handcuffed Warner.

"This is the easy part," he said.

"And it gets even easier," she told him.

"How?"

"Go and find Amanda and calm her down," said
Turnbull.

"But Turnbull, you know she likes . . ."

"Parker, do as I say. I am the boss remember!"

CHAPTER SEVEN

A few weeks later, Turnbull and Parker closed the case.
They were talking to Amanda and Mrs. Warner in the
kitchen of their house. Amanda was happy
and smiling.

"Amanda will need treatment for her sleepwalking. We know now that her father was giving her drugs that made her violent," Turnbull said.

"The drugs he gave you, Mrs. Warner, were slowly killing you," said Parker.

Mrs. Warner brushed a tear from her eye and hugged her daughter. "I knew something was wrong. I lied to myself for all those years. I have let Amanda down so badly."

Turnbull squeezed her arm. "Don't blame yourself. Look to the future."

Later that day, Parker and Turnbull were sitting in a cafe.

"I don't know what Amanda saw in you," laughed Turnbull. "Maybe she only liked you when she was on mind bending drugs."

"Give me a break, Laura!" Parker shouted.

"Oh it's Laura today, is it? Well, Mrs. Warner told me something else. She said Amanda tried to kill me because she thought you liked me. Now that is a laugh! You don't liked me, do you? I mean, we are just good buddies."

"Yeah, just buddies," he muttered.

"You got it," said Turnbull.

Then she got up and left him.

He looked just a little sad.

GLOSSARY OF TERMS

at a judge's pleasure in jail

FBI Federal Bureau of Investigation

fake something that is not genuine, a phoney

first degree murder very serious crime of killing

flattery insincere compliments

fuse box box containing safety devices for electricity circuits in a house

gambling debt money owed as a result of betting

honest truthful

life insurance policy money paid out when someone dies

nigh near

patients people in hospitals

preacher a clergyman

prime time the most expensive advertising time on TV

prisoners people held in jails

ratings the number of people watching a program

QUIZ

1. Who lives at number four Ronald Terrace?

2. What does Mr. Warner do?

3. Who sleepwalks?

4. Who did Agents Turnbull and Parker go to see at the hospital and why?

5. How much money does Mr. Warner owe?

6. How does Mr. Warner plan to repay his debts?

7. Who gets trapped in the cellar?

8. Who gets hit over the head?

9. Who got Mr. Warner in an armlock and swung him around?

10. What is Agent Turnbull's first name?

ABOUT THE AUTHOR

Paul Blum has taught for over twenty years in London inner city schools.

I wrote The Extraordinary Files for my students so they've been tested by some fierce critics (you)! That's why I know you'll enjoy reading them.

I've made the stories edgy in terms of character and content and I've written them using the kind of fast-paced dialogue you'll recognize from television shows. I hope you'll find The Extraordinary Files an interesting and easy to read collection of stories.

ANSWERS TO QUIZ

1. The Warners

2. He is a TV preacher.

3. Amanda Warner

4. Dr. Smith. He is a world expert on sleeping problems and they hoped he would help them with the Warner case.

5. $4,000,000

6. He plans to arrange for Amanda to kill Mrs. Warner so that he gets the money from Mrs. Warner's life insurance policy and Amanda gets sent to jail for life.

7. Agent Parker

8. Agent Turnbull

9. Agent Turnbull

10. Laura